Funny Faces,
Wacky Wings,
and other
Silly Big Bird
Things

Published by The Millbrook Press, Inc.
2 Old New Milford Road
Brookfield, CT   06804
www.millbrookpress.com

Cover photograph courtesy of Animals Animals
(© Dani/Jeske). Photographs courtesy of Photo
Researchers, Inc.: pp. 1 (© Art Wolfe), 2 (© Tim Davis), 5
(bottom: © Tim Davis), 8-9 (© Akira Uchiyama), 13 (©
George Bernard/SPL), 15 (© Art Wolfe), 19 (© Dr. M. P.
Kahl), 25 (© Art Wolfe), 29 (© Tom McHugh), 30 (© Phil
Dotson); © VIREO: pp. 3 (A. Mauviel), 4 (top: A. Morris;
bottom: Doug Wechsler), 5 (top right: H. & J. Eriksen),
10–11 (Rob Curtis), 17 (A. Cruickshank), 23 (J. Williams);
Bruce Coleman, Inc.: pp. 4 (center: © John Giustina), 5
(top left: © George Forrest), 7 (© Tuo De Roy), 20 (© K. &
K. Ammann), 21 (© Joe McDonald), 27 (© John Shaw);
Animals Animals: p. 26 (© Marian Bacon)

Library of Congress Cataloging-in-Publication Data
Copeland, Cynthia L.
Funny faces, wacky wings, and other silly big bird things / Cynthia L.
Copeland and Alexandra P. Lewis.
p. cm. — (Silly Millies)
Summary: Illustrations and easy text point out strange physical
characteristics or behaviors of certain large birds, such as ostriches,
bustards, grebes, and penguins.
ISBN 0-7613-2863-7 (lib. bdg.) — ISBN 0-7613-1788-0 (pbk.)
[1. Birds—Fiction.] I. Lewis, Alexandra P. II. Title. III. Series.
PZ7.C78797 Fu 2002   [Fic]—dc21   2002006031

silly Millies

Funny Faces, Wacky Wings, and other Silly Big Bird Things

Cynthia L. Copeland

Alexandra P. Lewis

The Millbrook Press
Brookfield, Connecticut

I can think of many words
that tell about all kinds of birds.
Words like

FEATHERS,

FLY,

and SING,

Words like LEG

and BEAK

and
WING.

These words and more are in this book.
Turn the page and take a look!

All blue-footed boobies

think their blue feet are neat.

They always show them off

to other boobies when they meet.

Two cranes bow and leap
and prance.
Flap their wings in a
lovey-dovey dance.

Boy crane says, "Here I am!
Look at me!"
Girl crane says, "Okay!
I see!"

The spoonbill's beak
is called a bill.
It looks just like
a spoon.
Sometimes she
would like a fork
to help her
eat her fill.

There once was a bird called a dodo.

It could not run, swim, or fly.

The dodo birds are all gone now—

is it any wonder why?

Black-bellied bustards do not
chirp or cheep.

They do not sing and they do not peep.

Bustards YELL! They shout it out!

What IS all the yelling about?

The pelican's pouch can carry fish
and it is also a dinner dish!
Fish for supper, fish for snack.
Is there nothing but fish inside
that sack?

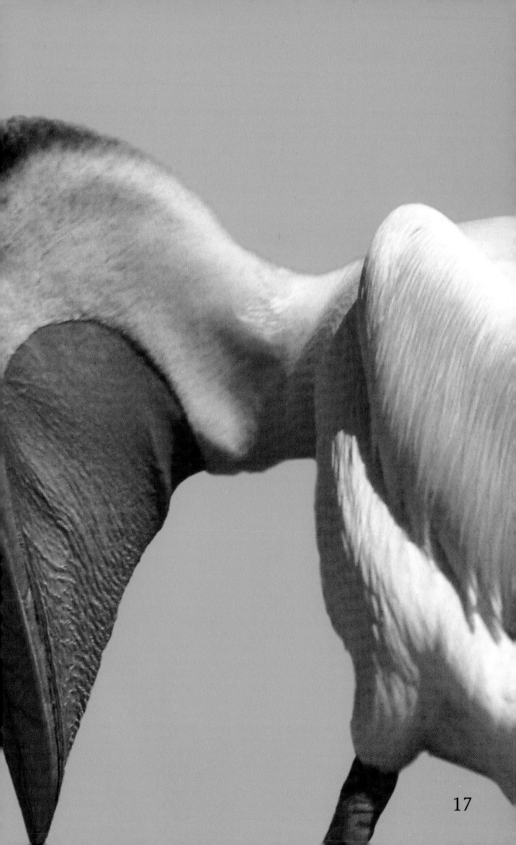

Baby Flamingo wants to see

just how hard that pose can be.

One leg balances,

one leg bends.

Okay! Now she can show her friends!

The ostrich
looks like an
eight-foot-tall
bowling ball—
with feathers.

He has legs that end
with just two toes
and a neck that goes and
goes and GOES.

In Owl's upside-down town

a frown is a smile,

a hole is a pile,

and a long time is just a little while.

Cassowary wears a very
silly helmet on his head.
He is a shy bird, a cannot fly bird,
a bird who can swim, instead.

Penguins are big silly birds,
falling willy-nilly birds,
sometimes a little bit
chilly birds.

This icy hillside is a thrill slide,

a zippy, slippy downhill chill ride!

When Condor is in a hungry mood,

he flies until he spies some food.

The bigger and deader

his dinner, the better!

Grebes dash, two by two, on top
of the lake.
What is wrong with their wings?
Did they make a mistake?

Someone should tell the grebe pairs
that are there
it is faster to take off and fly
in the air.

Dear Parents:

Congratulations! By sharing this book with your child, you are taking an important step in helping him or her become a good reader. *Funny Faces, Wacky Wings* is perfect for children who are beginning to read alone, either silently or aloud. Below are some ideas for making sure your child's reading experience is a positive one.

Tips for Reading
- First, read the book aloud to your child. Then, if your child is able to "sound out" the words, invite him or her to read to you. If your child is unsure about a word, you can help by asking, "What word do you think it might be?" or, "Does that make sense?" Point to the first letter or two of the word and ask your child to make that sound. If she or he is stumped, read the word slowly, pointing to each letter as you sound it out. Always provide lots of praise for the hard work your child is doing.
- If your child knows the words but is having trouble reading aloud, cut a plain white ruler-sized strip of paper to place under the line as your child reads. This will help your child keep track of his or her place.
- If your child is a beginning reader, have her or him read this book aloud to you. Reading and rereading is the best way to help any child become a successful reader.

Tips for Discussion
- On page 4–5 we list some bird words. Can the reader find those words in the book?
- The Dodo bird on page 12–13 is extinct. Does the reader know of any other animals that are extinct? He or she might enjoy learning about ancient extinct animals like the woolly mammoth and the saber-toothed tiger.

Lea M. McGee, Ed.D.
Professor, Literacy Education
University of Alabama

REVISED EDITION V

YOU CAN GROW ORCHIDS

By **MARY NOBLE**

Paintings by
Marion Ruff Sheehan

Published by:

MARY NOBLE McQUERRY
McQUERRY ORCHID BOOKS
Jacksonville, Florida USA

Fifth Edition, First Printing 1987
Produced in U.S.A.
ISBN 0-913928-06-2
Library of Congress Catalog Card Number 87-90685

PHOTOGRAPHS: Mary Noble McQuerry, Jack W. McQuerry, Louis O. Egner, Edwin S. Boyett, John K. Derbonne, Robert M. Steward, Eva Noble, D. C. Flynn, Stewart Orchids.

DRAWINGS: Marion R. Sheehan, Bruno Alberts. From The Orchid Album (1882–1897) by J. Nugent Fitch.

CONTENTS

Cattleyas are the most familiar orchids and are easy to grow if you understand their needs.

 This book is dedicated to
my husband, Jack W. McQuerry